This vacation Bible school inspired the Bible Buddy named Savanna. Savanna is a giraffe. Since giraffes are tall, they can reach food that other animals can't. Savanna helps kids remember all the ways that

God is good!

Best of Buddies
Good, Gooder, Goodest! Thank You, God!
Written by **JEFF WHITE** *and* **MIKAL KEEFER** *Illustrated by* **JULIE MELLAN**

Group | **lifetree**™

MyLifetree.com
Loveland, CO

Copyright © 2019 Group Publishing, Inc./0000 0001 0362 4853
Lifetree™ is an imprint of Group Publishing, Inc. Visit our website: **group.com**

Authors: Jeff White and Mikal Keefer
Illustrator: Julie Mellan
Chief Creative Officer: Joani Schultz
Senior Editor: Candace McMahan
Designer: RoseAnne Sather
Assistant Editor: Cherie Shifflett

Scripture quotations are taken from the Holy Bible, New Living Translation, copyright © 1996, 2004, 2015 by Tyndale House Foundation. Used by permission of Tyndale House Publishers, Inc., Carol Stream, Illinois 60188. All rights reserved.

Library of Congress Cataloging-in-Publication Data
Names: White, Jeff, 1968- author. | Keefer, Mikal, 1954- author. | Mellan,
  Julie, illustrator.
Title: Good, gooder, goodest! : thank you, God! / written by Jeff White and
  Mikal Keefer ; illustrated by Julie Mellan.
Description: Loveland, CO : Group Publishing, Inc., [2019] | Series: Best of
  buddies.
Identifiers: LCCN 2018041797 (print) | LCCN 2018048393 (ebook) | ISBN
  9781470757212 (ePub) | ISBN 9781470757267 (first American hardcover)
Classification: LCC PZ8.3.W58767 (ebook) | LCC PZ8.3.W58767 Goo 2019 (print)
  | DDC [E]--dc23
LC record available at https://lccn.loc.gov/2018041797

978-1-4707-5726-7 (hardcover)
978-1-4707-5721-2 (ePub)
Printed in China.
001 China 1218

10 9 8 7 6 5 4 3 2 1   28 27 26 25 24 23 22 21 20 19

There's so much in life that's far better than bad.
Creation's jam-packed with both happy and glad!

They're easy to miss when our lives get too tough
With skinned knees and lost toys and other sad stuff.

But when life is joyful (and it is—a lot!),
Shout "God is so good!" for the good things you've got!

God sends you good gifts—
they're yours to unwrap.
I'll help you notice.
I'll draw you a map!

Let's march through today
and see how God was true
when he promised good gifts
to me and to you.

And top of the list—
maybe it's understood—
we'll see that it's true
that our God is so good!

Just look at God's creatures—they'll bring you a grin.
Puppies and penguins and pink pangolins.

Baby goats bouncing and leaping like crazy,
Panda bears working so hard to be lazy.

Curlicue tails and funny, cold noses—
God's goodness is in everything he composes.

The bed that you sleep in, your blankets and sheets,
Soft, downy pillows and socks for your feet.

God gives you playthings like gizmos and games
And heartwarming days that get tucked in a frame.

For all the fun things in your life, just declare,
"My God is so good!" as loud as you dare.

For people who love you
with all of their heart,
who help you and love you
and tell you you're smart,

For kinfolk who keep you
from feeling alone,
for friends by your side
when you face the unknown,

For anyone part of your
feel-good squad—
they're very good gifts
from your very good God.

And when you get hungry, then God's got your back.
And your tummy, too—just check out these snacks!

Apples and biscuits and green beans and steak,
Plus extra-thick frosting on your birthday cake.

God makes your life tasty as tasty can be,
So open your mouth and say, "God's good to me!"

You've got a heart that keeps right on ticking
And two paws for waving and two paws for kicking.

God's tucked lots of smarts up there in your brain
And sends your blood flowing straight through your veins.

We aren't all the same, but when all's said and done,
Our God did good work making everyone!

Life feels so scrumptious when you stretch and stand
And go tiptoe barefoot across salty sand.

When you open your eyes to a bright, new sunrise
Then watch as clouds tumble new shapes in the sky.

God is the giver of flowers and woods,
So let's pause and thank him: "God you're so good!"

What could be better than making some art?
It's good for your head, and it's great for your heart.

So color or draw, sculpt granite or write,
Your art's a reflection of God's shining light.

God's a creator,
and when you are, too,
it says, "God is good!"
and he's living in you.

It's a very good day when smiles light up your face
And joy's what you're spreading all over the place.

Smiles are like sunshine shared straight from your soul.
Share one right now—let's get on a roll!

And if you need something to smile about,
Think, "My God is so good! Of that there's no doubt!"

Music is fun, and so's singing aloud.
Choirs are always the best kind of crowd.

Music is God's greatest
gift to our ears.
It's the height of delight
and makes fear disappear.

When life's feeling fine,
just break into song.
Sing, "God is so good!"
Sing it loud,
sing it strong!

Stories are what makes the whole world go 'round.
A good book will lift you when you're feeling down.

A day with a book? It's a good day, indeed!
And there's always another book ready to read.

God's book is the Bible—the best book of all.
It tells how God's good—in big ways and small.

There are
gazillions of good
things that I'd like to list:
bubbles and baubles and
blueberry twists.

Pancakes and pizzas,
parades and grand prizes,
plus pillows that come
in all shapes and all sizes.

Forts made of blankets
and blocks made of wood.
All given by God,
so let's say,
"God is good!"

It's God who's the goodest of all the good things.
He's the Friend of all friends and the King of all kings.

It's God who makes everything sparkle like new;
That's how he made me, and it's how he'll make you.

So say it now with me—just once more, again:
Our God is so good! (Can I get an "amen"?)

There are so many good things that come and then go
But one's here forever (and that's God, you know!).

So look for his smile in the gifts that he gives:
The joy that surrounds you, mistakes he forgives.

And I'd ask one favor, if only you would:
Always remember: **Our God is so good!**

"Remember the Lord,
who is great and glorious."

(Nehemiah 4:14)